This book is dedicated to Cole and Reese.
You fill me with so much joy and love.
Thank you for inspiring me.

ANNA
and the
SCANDINAVIAN
HEARTS

ANNA

words by

WENDY JANGAARD JENSEN

pictures by

KATHERINE CASTANO

"Anna, over here." Mom waved from across the playground.

"Mom!" She ran towards her familiar face.

Anna loved school. But she always looked forward to the end of each day. When the school bell rang, she could feel the energy and excitement all around her.

"How was your day?" Mom asked.

"It was fun," Anna replied.

"Today we talked about symbols."

"Symbols?" asked Mom.

"You know—like..

BIRDS,

STARS,

LEAVES,

AND SO MANY OTHERS

Symbols are the things around you that mean something special and make you feel a certain way."

"My teacher's favorite symbol is a rainbow," said Anna. "It reminds him of magic and makes him feel hopeful.

"And Dylan loves rocks. She keeps them in her pockets. She feels calm and happy when she holds them."

"What's your favorite
   symbol?" asked Mom.

"I'm not sure yet,"
   Anna said.

"Let's stop at Grandma's,"
Anna said with a smile.
"She loves it when we visit."

Grandma lived nearby so they spent a lot of time at her house. Anna's grandparents had moved from Norway and Sweden to the U.S. years ago.

Anna loved visiting their home. They had so many fun stories to share. And she thought their accents sounded so cool when they talked.

"Anna!" Grandma greeted them with warm hugs.
"I'm so happy to see you. How was your day?"

"It was fun, Grandma. We talked about symbols."

Grandma welcomed them into the kitchen.

"Would either of you like a drink or a cookie?" she asked.

Anna's grandma always had fresh coffee and homemade cookies. Anna thought Grandma's favorite symbol might be a cup of coffee.

Anna noticed how cozy and welcome she felt at grandma's house. Of course, it was because her grandma always made Anna feel special. But maybe it was more than that.

Anna looked around the room and noticed so many beautiful things.

Candles glowing, beautiful art..

..and colorful Dala horses. She saw so many special items from their heritage.

Then something else grabbed her attention—hearts. They were everywhere!

"Grandma, why do you have so many hearts?"

"They remind me of Sweden, and make me feel happy," said her grandma.

"Grandma," said Anna, "that's exactly what we learned about in school today!"

floral wreath

mid summer pole

folk dancing

"Can you show me some of your favorite things?" Anna asked.

"Of course, I'd love to!" Her grandma stood and looked around the room.

Anna could see the smile growing on her face while noticing all her special things.

Grandma reached for her candle holder.

"In Sweden, the winters are dark.
So, people light candles in their homes."

"At night you can see candles in the windows throughout the neighborhood, it's so beautiful and welcoming."

Grandpa walked into the room.

"Are you sharing your favorite things?" he asked.

"Yes, what's yours?" asked Mom.

"My sweater, of course. This is a Norwegian sweater. It keeps me warm on the cold nights fishing in Alaska," Grandpa said in a strong, confident voice.

Anna noticed small
hearts in the pattern
of his sweater.

Anna could listen to her grandparents talk all evening. She thought of how brave they must have been to leave their homes. Anna knew how proud they were to share their stories.

"Thanks for sharing," Anna said, as they all hugged goodbye. She already looked forward to her next visit.

At home that night she looked around her room and noticed so many hearts. Large hearts and small hearts—hearts in so many colors!

Anna felt relief, she knew for certain what her favorite symbol was.

It was hearts!

Anna smiled, thinking about Grandma and how
hearts made her feel connected to their heritage.
Hearts made Anna feel happy too.

Anna's mind swirled with excitement when she thought about going to school the next day. She could hardly wait to share her love of hearts and tell the class why they held so much meaning for her!

Do you have a favorite symbol?

How does it make you feel?

About the Author: The Anna book series is inspired by Wendy's Scandinavian heritage. Her family celebrates traditions that were brought to the U.S. from her grandparents, cousins, and aunts/uncles when they immigrated from Norway and Sweden. Wendy is proud to share her love of hearts and her Scandinavian Heritage with you in a way that brings to life the joy and stories of her family. Stay tuned for more Anna stories . . .

About the Book: Follow Anna's journey to discovering her heritage – and ignite your passion for discovering your own along the way. Meet Anna, an ordinary little girl who is about to learn the magic of the little and big things around her when she's faced with the big question – "what do different symbols mean to you?"

We see her transformation, how she grows more aware of the hearts and symbols in her surroundings, and how this deepens her connection to her roots. Anna's encounters ignite the passion and desire to learn about the heritage and the benefits that come with it, such as a sense of belonging and a deeper appreciation of where we come from.

These pages are beautifully illustrated and carry a profound message that your child will love!

Stay tuned for more Anna stories . . .

Book Title: Anna and the Scandinavian Hearts
Written by: Wendy Jangaard Jensen / Illustrated by: Katherine Castano

Copyright © 2022 by Scandinavian Hearts, Wendy Jangaard Jensen

For more information go to: www.ScandinavianHearts.com

Free Gift for My Readers ♡

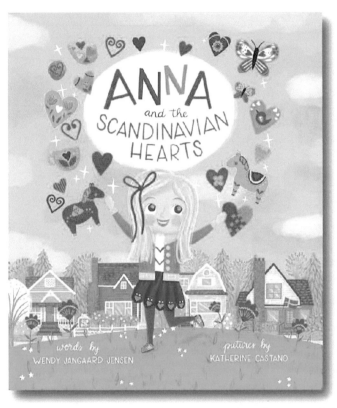

Would you like to make your own Scandinavian Heart?

A fun free activity for the family! (A $5.99 value)

The perfect way to add your favorite symbol to your home. Enjoy your gift.

Scan the QR code above with your smartphone or tablet.
Or, go to www.ScandinavianHearts.com/freegift

Made in United States
Troutdale, OR
12/11/2023

15707370R00021